Knick Knack Paddy Whack

illustrated by
Christiane Engel
sung by
SteveSongs

Barefoot Books
Celebrating Art and Story

This old man,
he played one,
He played Knick Knack
on his drum.

With a Knick Knack, Paddy Whack
give a dog a bone,
This old man came rolling home.

With a Knick Knack, Paddy Whack
give a dog a bone,
This old man came rolling home.

This old man,
he played **three**,
He played Knick Knack
happily.

With a Knick Knack, Paddy Whack
give a dog a bone,
This old man came rolling home.

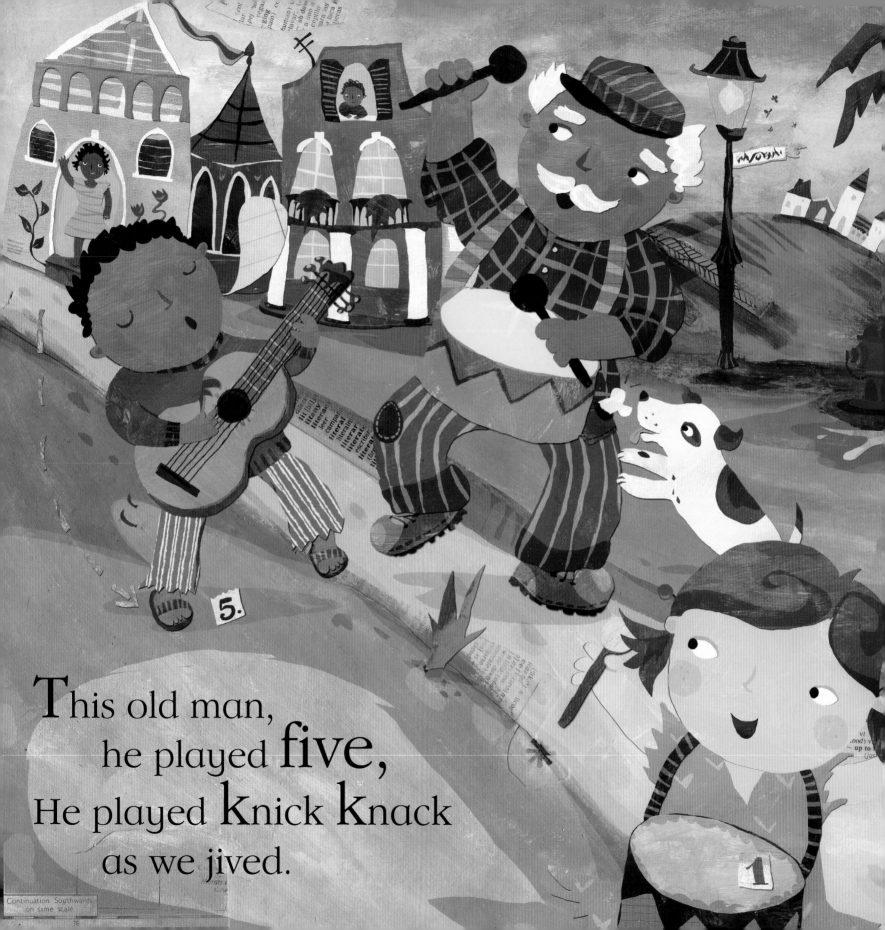

This old man,
he played five,
He played Knick Knack
as we jived.

With a Knick Knack, Paddy Whack
give a dog a bone,
This old man came rolling home.

This old man, he played six,
He played knick knack on the bricks.

This old man, he played seven,
He played Knick Knack by the oven.

This old man, he played eight,
He played Knick Knack as we ate.

This old man, he played nine,
He played Knick Knack all the time.

With a Knick Knack, Paddy Whack
give a dog a bone,
This old man came rolling home.

With a Knick Knack, Paddy Whack
give a dog a bone,
This old man came rolling home.

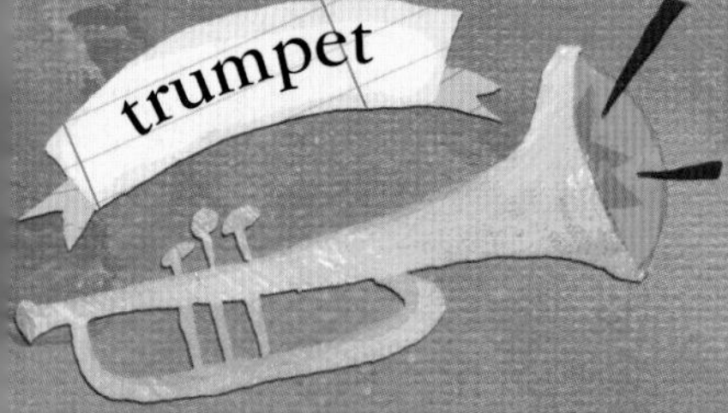

Instrument Families

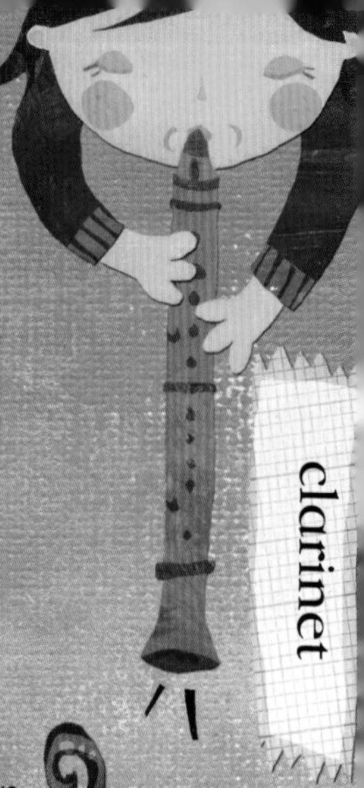

trumpet

drums

maracas

clarinet

Musical instruments belong to different groups, or families. They are grouped together because of the kinds of sounds they make. Here are the instrument families you can see in this book:

Brass instruments have a bell-shaped opening at one end. In this book, the **trombone** and **trumpet** belong to the brass family. Other members of the brass family include the French horn and the tuba.

Woodwind instruments used to be made of wood, but now are made from metals and plastics as well. The player makes the sounds by blowing air into the instrument. In this book, the **clarinet** and the **saxophone** belong to the woodwind family. Other members of this family are the oboe, piccolo and flute.

bass

Stringed instruments are bowed, plucked or strummed to make the sounds. You can see the stringed **bass** and **guitar** in this book. Violins, violas and cellos also belong to the string family.

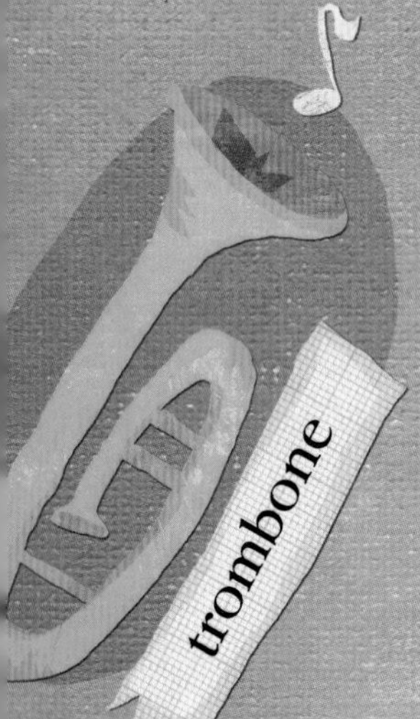

Percussion instruments are struck or shaken to create a sound. The family is divided into untuned (non-pitched) percussion, like the **drums** and **maracas** in this book, and tuned (pitched) percussion, such as the xylophone or timpani.

trombone

saxophone

Keyboard instruments have bars, pipes or strings that vibrate when a player presses down on the keys. There is an **electric keyboard** in this book; pipe organs, accordions and pianos also belong to this family.

keyboard

guitar

Sing Along

This old man,   he played **one**,   He played knick knack   on his drum. With a

Knick Knack, Paddy Whack   give a dog a bone,   This old man came rolling   home.

This old man, he played **two**, he played knick knack just for you . . .

This old man, he played **three**, he played knick knack happily . . .

This old man, he played **four**, he played knick knack on my door . . .

This old man, he played **five**, he played knick knack as we jived . . .

This old man, he played **six**, he played knick knack on the bricks . . .

This old man, he played **seven**, he played knick knack by the oven . . .

This old man, he played **eight**, he played knick knack as we ate . . .

This old man, he played **nine**, he played knick knack all the time . . .

This old man, he played **ten**, if you sing a bit louder, we'll do it all again!

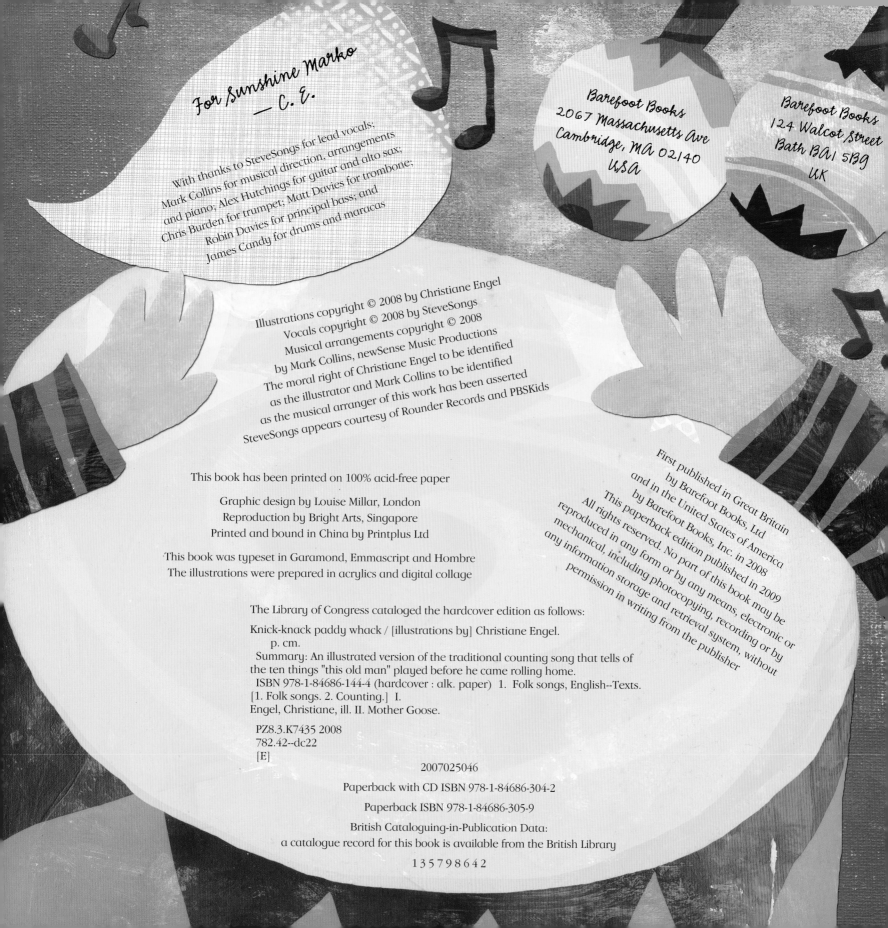

For Sunshine Marko
— C. E.

With thanks to SteveSongs for lead vocals;
Mark Collins for musical direction, arrangements
and piano; Alex Hutchings for guitar and alto sax;
Chris Burden for trumpet; Matt Davies for trombone;
Robin Davies for principal bass; and
James Candy for drums and maracas

Barefoot Books
2067 Massachusetts Ave
Cambridge, MA 02140
USA

Barefoot Books
124 Walcot Street
Bath BA1 5BG
UK

This book has been printed on 100% acid-free paper

Graphic design by Louise Millar, London
Reproduction by Bright Arts, Singapore
Printed and bound in China by Printplus Ltd

This book was typeset in Garamond, Emmascript and Hombre
The illustrations were prepared in acrylics and digital collage

First published in Great Britain
by Barefoot Books, Ltd
and in the United States of America
by Barefoot Books, Inc. in 2008
This paperback edition published in 2009

The Library of Congress cataloged the hardcover edition as follows:

Knick-knack paddy whack / [illustrations by] Christiane Engel.
   p. cm.
   Summary: An illustrated version of the traditional counting song that tells of
the ten things "this old man" played before he came rolling home.
   ISBN 978-1-84686-144-4 (hardcover : alk. paper) 1. Folk songs, English--Texts.
[1. Folk songs. 2. Counting.] I.
Engel, Christiane, ill. II. Mother Goose.

PZ8.3.K7435 2008
782.42--dc22
[E]

                        2007025046

Paperback with CD ISBN 978-1-84686-304-2

Paperback ISBN 978-1-84686-305-9

British Cataloguing-in-Publication Data:
a catalogue record for this book is available from the British Library

1 3 5 7 9 8 6 4 2